ROCK 'N ROAR

By Justine Korman
Illustrated by John Costanza

A Golden Book • New York
Western Publishing Company, Inc., Racine, Wisconsin 53404

Montana Max roared onto the Acme Looniversity
soccer field in his Acme All-Special Vehicle.

"Get your kicks somewhere else!" he snarled at Buster
Bunny and Babs Bunny.

The bunnies weren't about to stop their game. But
Max flipped a switch, a special horn popped out, and a
blast of air blew Buster off the field.

"Good thing I've got a piece of the rock," Buster quipped, peeling himself off the rock where he had landed—hard!

His soccer ball rolled into a deep, dark hole. Buster followed the ball and found...

...a huge cave with stalactites hanging from the ceiling.

"I had no idea soccer was this popular in Acme Acres," Buster said upon seeing a heap of soccer balls covering the floor.

"Buster, what are you doing down there?" Babs called from above. "It's time to go home."

Buster grabbed a ball and scrambled out.

Back home, Buster studied Ancient Acme History while spinning his soccer ball with his ears.

"Let's see," Buster muttered. "There was the Acme Tea Party, then the signing of the Acme Constitution..."

Suddenly the ball slipped, bounced off the wall, rolled under the bed, and back out again. The "ball" cracked open. A cute baby Tyrannosaurus rex popped out and said, "Mama."

"Wow! A real baby dinosaur! And you're all mine!" Buster marveled. "This is great."

Buster named his new pet Rover. He quickly realized that Rover was hungry. And when a Tyrannosaurus rex is hungry, you don't keep him waiting. Buster emptied everything in the refrigerator into Rover's mouth—including the refrigerator!

Rover grew very fast. By the next morning he was 20
feet tall. Buster tried to explain that Rover had to stay
home while he went to school. But as soon as Buster was
gone, Rover felt lonely. So he followed Buster.

First Rover stomped through Babs's flower garden.
When he got to the Acme Acres Forest, he began to eat—
the trees! Eating all those trees made Rover thirsty, so he
drank Plucky Duck's swamp.

Babs and Plucky ran to the school, shrieking, "Monster!"

"Rover's no monster," Buster explained. "He's my pet."

Babs suggested that Buster's pet needed obedience school—and a breath mint!

When Montana Max saw Rover at school, he threw a
tantrum.

"It's not fair—I'm supposed to be the first kid on the
block to own anything, especially a dinosaur!" Max
fumed. "I gotta have it."

Buster took Babs's suggestion and immediately enrolled Rover in Acme Obedience Training. But this made more of an impression on the teacher, Foghorn Leghorn, than on Rover. When he told Rover to "sit," Foghorn found himself "feeling mighty low."

After school, Buster, Babs, Plucky, and Rover walked to Buster's home. They didn't see Montana Max and his butler, Grovely, setting a tasty trap for the hungry dinosaur. But Rover smelled chocolate cake.

Buster, Babs, and Plucky went inside Buster's home, and Rover wandered off toward the delicious smell of cake. While he stuffed his face, a steel-cabled net fell over him.

"People will pay a bundle to see a real dinosaur," Max said gloatingly. "I'll be even richer than my parents."

But Rover broke free and ran off looking for Buster, his "Mama."

"I'll sue!" Max shrieked. "That Acme Dinosaur Trap was guaranteed."

Buster and the gang came back outside, only to discover that Rover was gone.

"A classic case of Dinosaur Disappearance!" Plucky raved.

"Yes, Watson. This could make for a long, detailed search," Babs replied like a detective.

"Look!" said Buster, pointing to Rover's head on the horizon. "There's Rover. Mama's coming, baby!"

Buster found Rover wearing the remains of a flower shop.

"Rover's a little out of place in Acme Acres," Babs said.

"Aw, you guys are exaggerating," Buster protested.

Just then Montana Max's biplane zoomed overhead. Rover and the gang raced for the woods, pursued by the buzzing biplane.

The gang reached the entrance to the cave where Buster had found Rover's egg. They all scrambled in, but Rover got stuck halfway inside the entrance.

"They can't hide from me in my plane," Max said with a laugh. "They'll never defeat my Acme Arsenal. I'll get Buster and Babs out of the way and then that dino will be mine! People will pay big bucks to see it. I'm...out of gas?!"

Max's sputtering plane crashed into Rover's hefty back-end, driving the dinosaur into the cave.

Rover tumbled into the cave, shaking the walls. He stopped just short of the soccer-ball-shaped eggs.

"You'll be safe down here," Buster assured Rover.

"This is where I found Rover's egg," he told the others.

"Look at all the other eggs," said Babs. "We almost had dinosaur omelette on the menu," she joked, pushing the eggs away from Rover.

"Wait," said Buster. "More dinosaur eggs means..."

"More dinosaurs!" they all finished together.

"But where?" Buster asked.

Rover roared and the wall rumbled and shook, rattled and rolled. Bright light streamed in through cracks in the wall—it was sliding open!

The gang gaped at a prehistoric paradise full of dinosaurs.

"I never did believe that dinosaurs are extinct," Buster said.

"When you roared, it must have made the walls open. This is where you belong," he told Rover.

Rover did not want to say good-bye to his "Mama."

"Stay here with your dinosaur family and friends," Buster said and everyone's eyes filled with tears. "If you stay with me, Max will hunt you for the rest of your life," Buster explained.

Rover walked into the dinosaur world and roared again.

The wall slid shut as he waved good-bye.

After the wall had closed, Max popped down into the cave. He clutched his Acme Shrinking Shotgun and boasted, "I'll cut that monster down to size with one quick blast of my shrinking shotgun. Where's that dinosaur?" he demanded.

"What dinosaur? We just came down here to get my soccer ball," Buster said coolly. He grabbed a ball and started tossing it in the air.

"You can't pull the cashmere over my eyes," Montana Max blustered. "I know there's a dinosaur down here."

Rover roared behind the wall, which began to move again. Max fired his Shrinking Shotgun, which promptly shrank. Terrified, Max took to the sky... without his plane!

Back in his bedroom, Buster studied while spinning the soccer ball with his ears. The ball suddenly took off and bounced around the room. It cracked open and a baby girl dinosaur popped out.

"Mama!" the dinosaur chirped.

"Here we go again," Buster said with a sigh.

"Now wait a minute," Buster said. "If you're not my soccer ball, then where is it?"